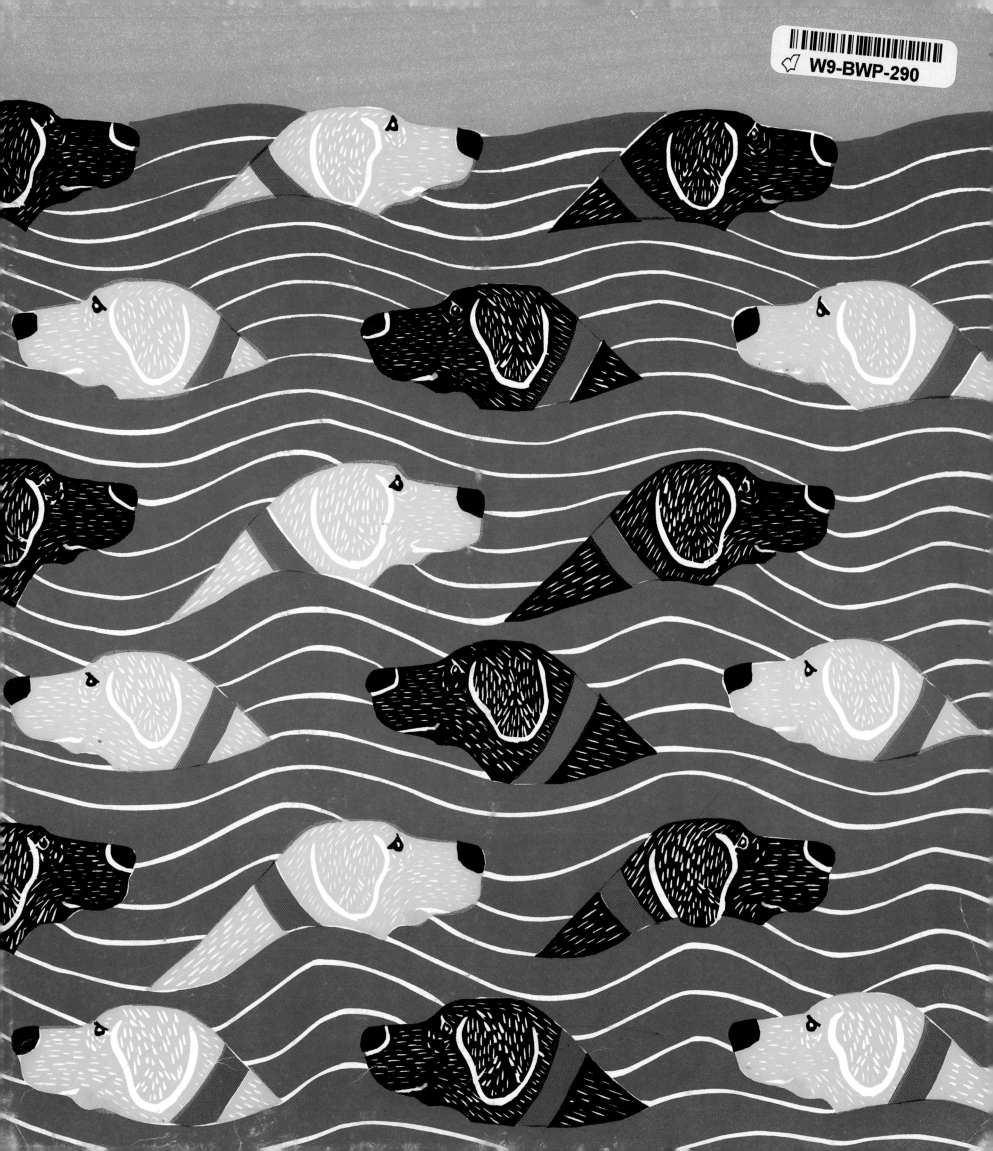

Sally Goes to the Beach

Written and Illustrated by

Stephen Huneck

Abrams Books for Young Readers
New York

Acknowledgments

I wish to thank Paul Gottlieb for his vision, my editor, Howard Reeves, for opening up a whole new world to me, and Lia Ronnen, whose charm and enthusiasm made working on this book even more fun. My thanks to Chantel Amey and Mike Lamp for their invaluable assistance, a special thanks to my wonderful wife Gwen and our three "girls," Sally, Dottie, and Heidi, for inspiring me, and finally, to Jim and Lynn Bryant for their friendship and support.

Artist's Note

To create a woodcut print, I first draw the design of the future print in crayon, laying out the prospective shapes and colors. I then carve one block of wood for each color in the appropriate shape. The result is a series of carved blocks, one for each color in the print. After a block has been inked with its respective color, acid-free archival paper is laid onto the block and hand rubbed. I repeat the process for each color block. When this process is completed, I then hang the prints to dry.—S.H.

You may visit Stephen Huneck's website at: www.dogmt.com

Original font design by Stephen Huneck

Designer: Ellen Nygaard Ford

Library of Congress Cataloging-in-Publication Data
Huneck, Stephen.
Sally goes to the beach / written & illustrated by Stephen Huneck.
p. cm.
SUMMARY: Sally, a black Labrador retriever, goes to the beach,
where she enjoys various activities with other visiting dogs.
ISBN 978-0-8109-4186-1
1. Dogs Juvenile fiction. [1. Dogs Fiction.
2. Beaches Fiction.] I. Title.
PZ10.3.H88   Sal 2000
[E]—dc21   99-28421

Printed and bound in China
19 18 17 16 15 14 13 12

Abrams Books for Young Readers are available at special discounts when purchased in quantity
for premiums and promotions as well as fundraising or educational use. Special editions can
also be created to specification. For details, contact specialmarkets@abramsbooks.com or the
address below.

eBook and app versions of Sally Goes to the Beach as well as other Sally titles are
distributed by Trajectory, Inc., and are available online.

ABRAMS
THE ART OF BOOKS SINCE 1949

115 West 18th Street
New York, NY 10011
www.abramsbooks.com

To Sally,
may we have many more
wonderful adventures
together.

Something is happening.
I can feel it in the air.

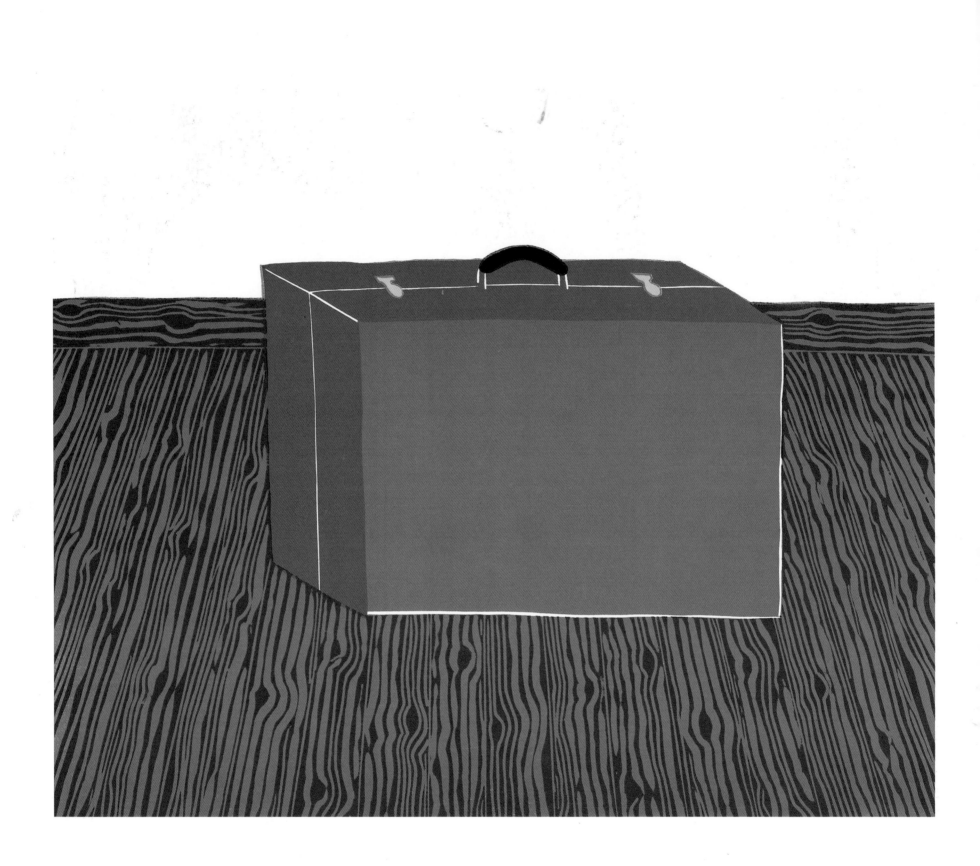

Then I see the suitcase.
We are going away.
We are going on vacation.

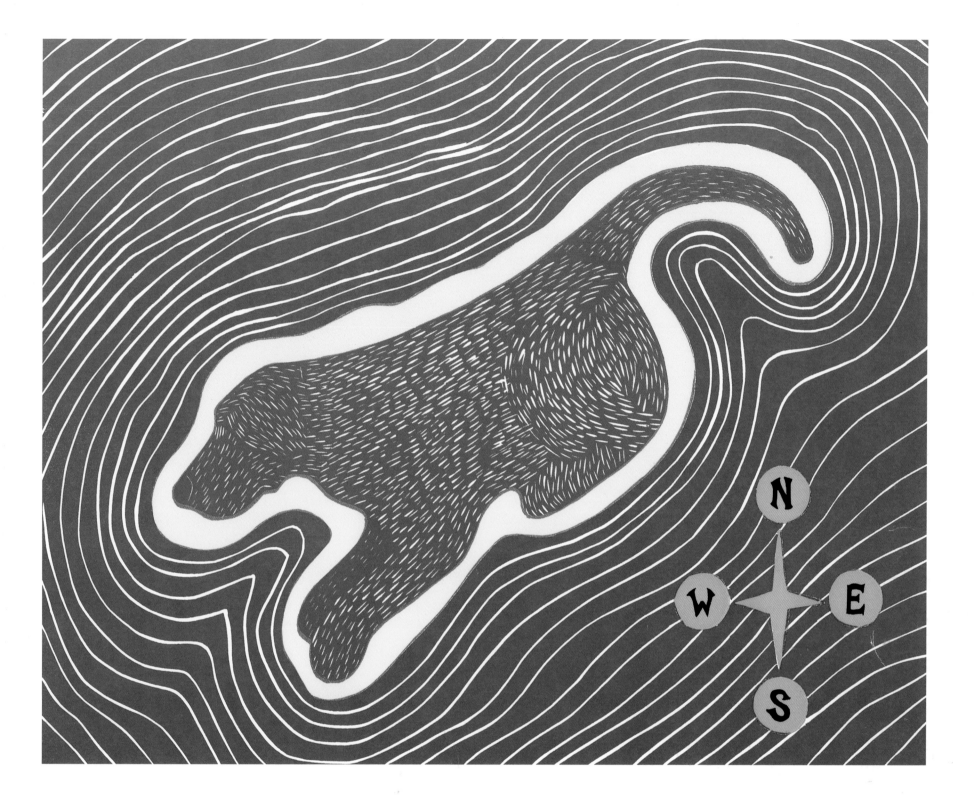

We are going to an island in the ocean.
We will take a ferry boat to get there.
And the best part is, it is a real dog place.

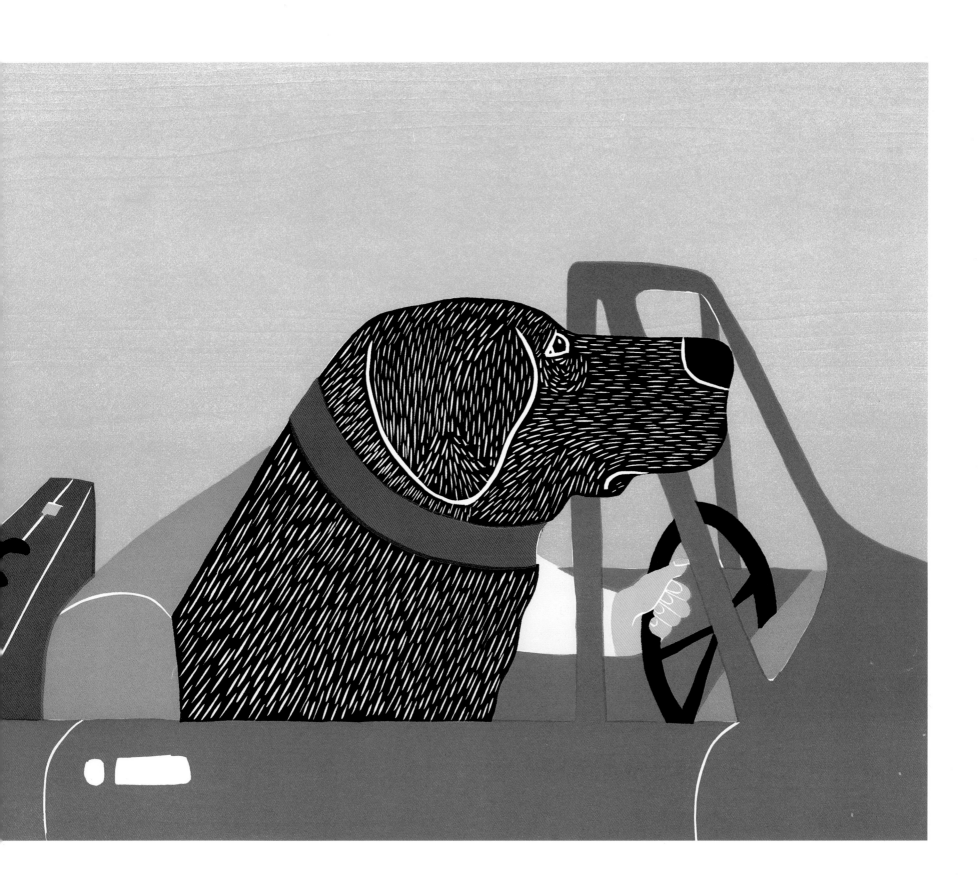

We pack the car and drive to the ferry.

We get on board.

I meet lots of dogs.

I see a bird. I see a boat.

I even see a whale.

I do not see the captain,
but I can imagine what he looks like.

Soon it is time to go ashore.

We share a cab to the cottage.

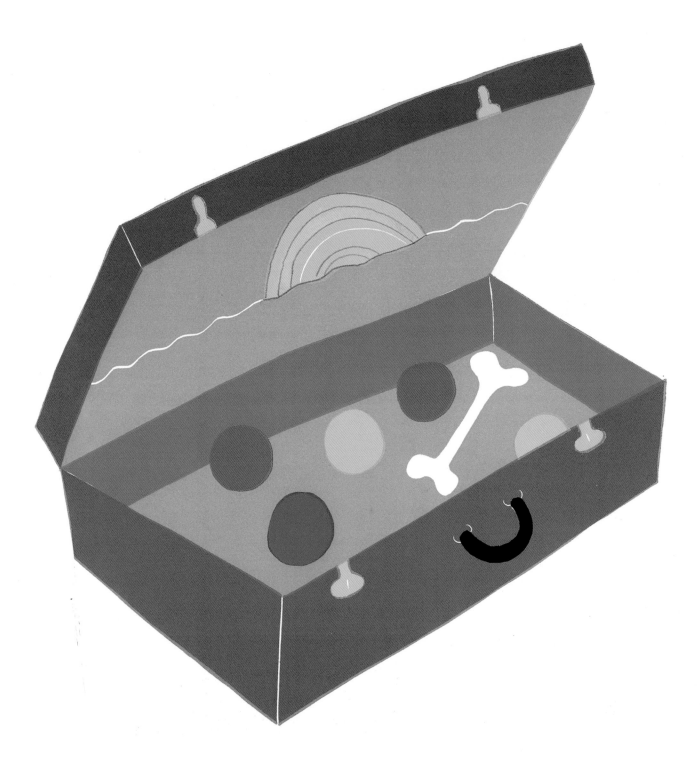

We unpack and go straight to the beach.

The sky is blue, and the sun is hot.

The air smells great, just like cat food!

We play in the ocean.

We ride in a boat.

Then I go exploring.

I realize right away,

I still have a lot to learn.

I am having so much fun,

I am sorry when the sun sets.

Until . . . I hear the can opener.

After dinner we do the dishes.

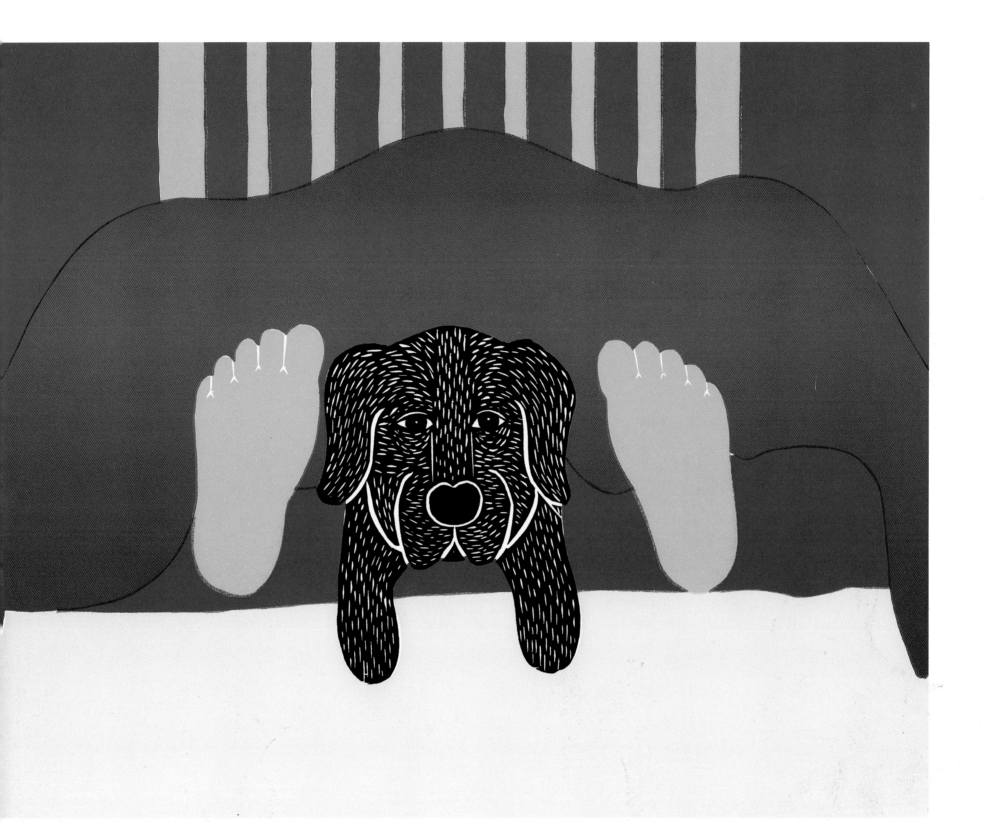

I cannot wait for tomorrow!

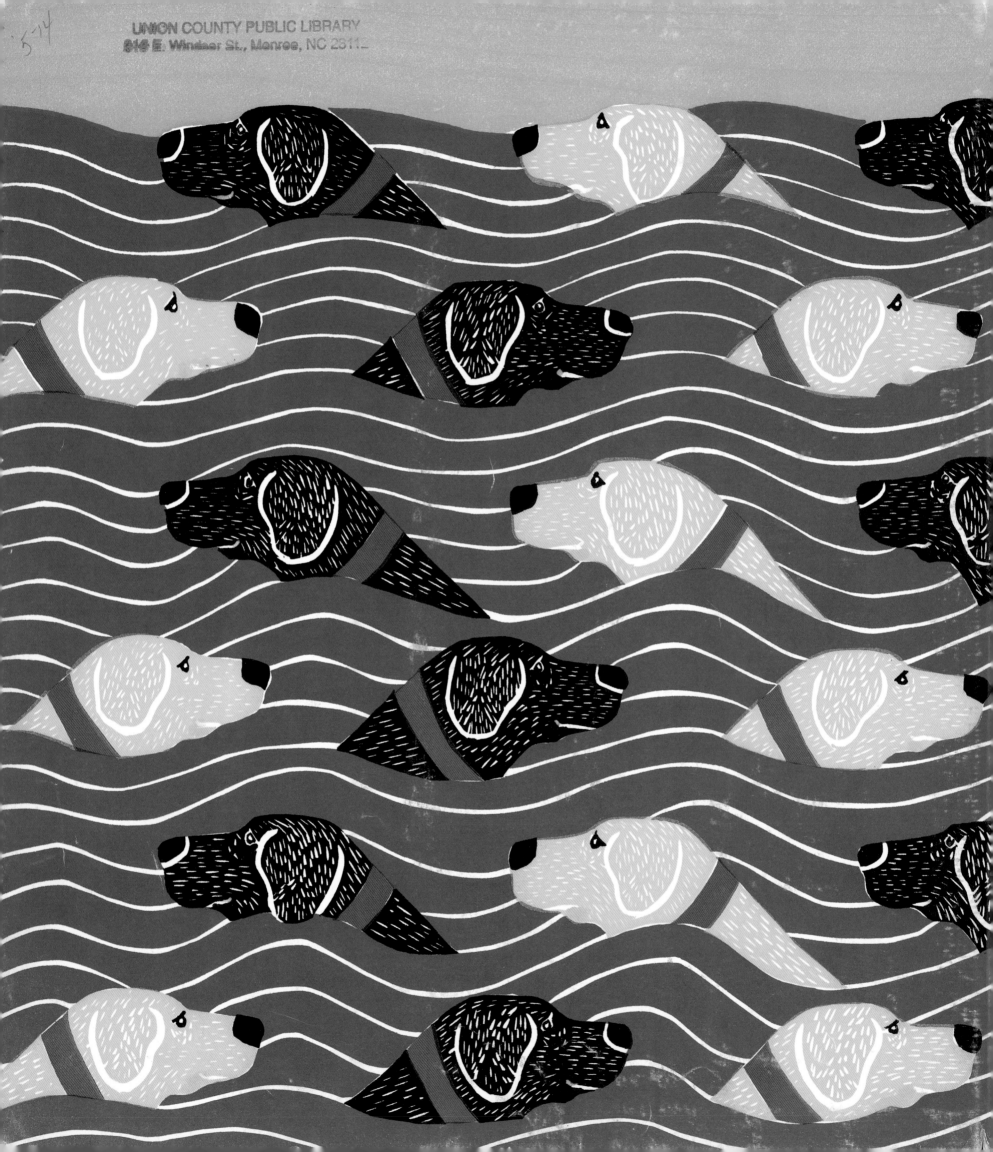